SPOOK SCHOOL

HORROR FROM THE DEEP

D0241066

For my nephew Harry, who is
an expert on octopuses ~ PJ

For Ethan, you're too young to read just yet,
but still, this one's for you! ~ TP

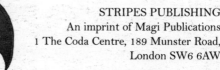

STRIPES PUBLISHING
An imprint of Magi Publications
1 The Coda Centre, 189 Munster Road,
London SW6 6AW

A paperback original
First published in Great Britain in 2010

Text copyright © Pete Johnson, 2010
Illustrations copyright © Tom Percival, 2010

ISBN: 978-1-84715-121-6

The right of Pete Johnson and Tom Percival to be identified
as the author and illustrator of this work respectively has
been asserted by them in accordance with the Copyright,
Designs and Patents Act, 1988.

All rights reserved.

This book is sold subject to the condition that it shall not, by way
of trade or otherwise, be lent, resold, hired out, or otherwise
circulated without the publisher's prior consent in any form
of binding or cover other than that in which it is published
and without a similar condition, including this condition,
being imposed upon the subsequent purchaser.

A CIP catalogue record for this book is available
from the British Library.

Printed and bound in the UK.

1 2 3 4 5 6 7 8 9 10

SPOOK SCHOOL

HORROR FROM THE DEEP

PETE JOHNSON

Illustrated by Tom Percival

Collect all the
Spook School titles:

LAIR OF THE MOTHMAN
Curse of the Rat-beast

KENT
LIBRARIES & ARCHIVES
C153882219

Chapter One

On the Ghost Train

Flying out of the coffin came a skeleton.

It let out a blood-curdling wail:

Waaaaa!

And for a moment, everyone on the ghost train shivered with fear. Then they clapped and cheered. If only they'd known that stretched out on the back seat were two *real* ghosts.

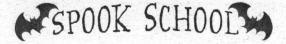

That's me, Charlie, and my best friend, Lewis. And we'd rather be called spooks, because it's much cooler! We go to Spook School where we have to do lessons every night. But they're not boring lessons. We learn brilliant things, like how to walk through doors and make things appear out of the air.

Lewis and I are also members of Spook Squad, a special group of spooks who come back to Earth to solve very scary, ghostly mysteries. But right now, Lewis and I were back on Earth for a holiday at the seaside. This was our reward for solving the incredible case of the Rat-beast. It was late afternoon when we arrived, and first of all we decided to visit the fair.

Of course, we had to take a ride on the ghost train. It hurtled past all these creepy figures yelling "Wooo!" and "Waaah!" and "Wooo, waaah!". Everyone was having a great spooky time until this boy jumped up and yelled, "This ghost train is rubbish. It's not scary at all!"

One of the children who was sitting with him cried, "Shut up, Andrew. Why have you got to spoil everything?"

But Andrew just shrugged. "I think all ghosts are rubbish. They're not even real."

Talk about rude! I was furious, but I didn't dare say a word. No one could see the two of us, but if we started talking, they'd hear us all right.

8

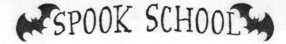

Andrew went on and on about how pathetic ghosts were, until the ghost train swayed to a halt and all the passengers clattered off.

"I think it's time we taught him some manners," I whispered to Lewis.

Lewis nodded.

We flew over and hovered just above Andrew's head. His friends had all run off and left him. He called after them but they just ignored him. Instead they queued up to go on the big wheel. Clearly even they were sick and tired of him. And it wasn't hard to see why.

I leaned down and whispered in his ear, "Hey, Stink-face."

Andrew jumped about three metres in the air. "Who said that?" he cried.

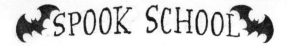

"Me," I replied.

Andrew looked all around him.

"Where are you?"

"Right here."

Lewis began to giggle.

"But where?" shrieked Andrew.

"I can't see anyone. Who's doing this?"

"Me," I said.

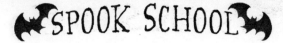

"This is such a silly trick," said Andrew. "I suppose you're with the fair."

"Noooo, I'm with the Spook Squad."

Then I decided it was time for Andrew to see me. So I closed my eyes and said, "See me, Andrew" twice. And suddenly I was floating right in front of his face.

I grinned at him. "Hi, how are you doing, Pongy-pants? I'm Charlie."

Andrew's jaw dropped. "You … you … how did you do that?" he spluttered.

"Very easily … I'm a ghost."

Then Lewis started to laugh uncontrollably. Andrew couldn't see him, but he could hear Lewis's gales of laughter all right.

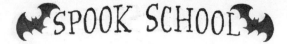

"And who's that?" he cried.

"Oh, that's just my mate Lewis," I said. "He's a ghost too. And we didn't like you calling us rubbish and saying we're not real. As you can see, I'm very real indeed and not rubbish at all. So come on, apologize."

But Andrew just gave a loud shriek, "Aaaaarrrggh", and sped away as fast as his legs would carry him.

"Now, why did he do that?" I muttered. "And anyway, I thought he didn't believe in ghosts." Lewis and I flew right up into the air, laughing.

"Wasn't that brilliant?" I cried.

"Fantastic," agreed Lewis. "It's a shame Andrew totally spoilt the ghost train though."

"But we can go back whenever we want," I said. "We're on holiday for two weeks. Come on, let's hit the beach."

A few minutes later we were staring out at the endless sea. Spook School is great, but there's no sea there. And we'd missed it. For a few seconds Lewis and I watched the water as it rose and fell with great gusty sighs. I took a deep sniff. I'd missed the tang of the sea too.

Then we started chasing about on top of the waves. No one could see us, of course. Not even the seagulls, whirling above our heads. It was getting dark now, and normally Lewis and I would be starting lessons at Spook School, but instead we could do whatever we wanted.

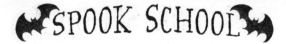

"This is going to be a top holiday," began Lewis. "What shall we do n…" He groaned. "Oh no, look."

Hovering above the waves was Spookmaster.

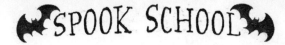

He was the headmaster of our school and very fierce indeed. He loomed in front of us in his large, flapping gown.

"What do you think he wants?" asked Lewis nervously.

"Maybe he'd like us to get him a stick of rock," I said. "Or perhaps he's got a new mystery for us to solve."

"He doesn't look very happy," said Lewis.

We started floating towards him. But he shook his head and pointed at Lewis.

"I think he just wants to see me," gulped Lewis.

"Fine," I said. "I'll wait for you on the beach."

Lewis nodded, and flew off towards Spookmaster as fast as he could.

15

Chapter Two

A Cry for Help

As I watched Lewis and Spookmaster
talking, I felt a bit cross that I hadn't
been invited too. Spookmaster flew right
up into the dark sky and hovered over
Lewis like a giant bird. He seemed really
angry about something. At last Lewis
came back looking very serious indeed.
I looked around for Spookmaster, but
he had vanished as suddenly and
mysteriously as he had appeared.

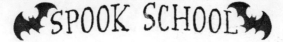

"It's all your fault," said Lewis grumpily.

"What is?"

"Spookmaster's just given me a right telling-off."

"He came all the way to Earth just to tell you off?" I asked.

"He was visiting Earth anyway," said Lewis, "and found out about you scaring Andrew."

"You're joking," I said.

"No, Spookmaster said we must never scare people for our own amusement, or call them 'Stink-face', or 'Pongy-pants'. And we must only let humans see us in emergencies. We should have just ignored what that boy said."

17

Lewis's voice began to wobble. "Spookmaster said I was in charge, so I'm completely to blame – and he was very disappointed in me. Not a single word of complaint about you, though."

I started to laugh.

"It's not funny, Charlie," he shouted.

"Oh, chill out, Lewis – anyway, you were laughing at Andrew too."

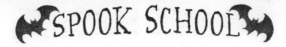

But Lewis ignored this and said huffily, "All you do is get me into trouble. I'm sick of you. Why have you always got to show off?"

"Will you just shut up," I snapped, "because you're really annoying me now."

Lewis didn't answer; instead he flew off in a strop. What a horrible, rotten start to our holiday this was. Well, Lewis could sulk if he wanted, I was going back to the fair.

I watched people in the hall of mirrors, and at the shooting gallery trying to win a goldfish. I rode on the waltzers and I even took another trip on the ghost train. But it wasn't any fun on my own. After about half an hour, I flew back to the beach.

I spotted Lewis right away. He was
staring out at the sea, looking fed up.
I flew over and hovered beside him,
watching the waves. I didn't say
anything and he didn't turn round,
but suddenly I could hear crying.

"Oh, you big cry-baby," I said.

Lewis swirled round. "I'm not
crying!"

But someone was.

Sobs that were growing louder and
louder.

Then we heard a voice say, "Oh, Lily,
please don't cry."

"I'm sorry, but I can't help it,"
wailed a girl.

Our quarrel forgotten, Lewis and
I flew over to a boy and girl about

20

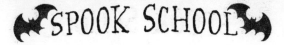

our age. They were dressed in really strange clothes. The boy was wearing short knee-length trousers, long knitted socks, a very worn looking shirt and jacket, and lace-up shoes. The girl was also wearing old-fashioned clothes, and lace-up shoes, as well as a funny blue hat. And they both had labels round their necks, with their names on: John and Lily. We could tell at once they were ghosts, as they were floating above the sand.

"Hi there," I said. They looked up, startled. "You're making a right racket. We could hear you halfway down the beach. What are you blubbing about?"

"Tactful as ever," murmured Lewis, rolling his eyes. Then he said, "I'm

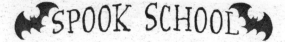

Lewis and this is Charlie. Maybe we can help."

The boy smiled suddenly and even the girl stopped crying. "I'm John and this is my sister, Lily," he said, "and we've been ghosts since World War II." That explained their old-fashioned clothes.

"We learned a bit about World War II at my old school," I said. "Were you caught up in one of the bombing raids?"

"Yes, in Sheffield," said John. "We should have been evacuated, but we didn't want to leave our home. And then the bombs came." He gave a deep sigh, and then asked, "Do you haunt near here?"

22

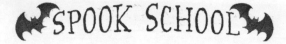

"No, we're super-cool ghosts, called spooks," I said. "And we're part of Spook Squad, which comes to Earth to solve really weird and scary mysteries. But we're on holiday at the moment."

"You must be very clever then," said Lily, suddenly gazing at me hopefully.

"Oh yeah, we are," I said confidently. "Especially me."

"But I'm in charge of all the missions," said Lewis, firmly. "So tell me, what's upsetting you?"

"Well, the thing is," Lily explained, "we've found it very hard to settle anywhere. In fact, we've been looking for somewhere to haunt for about seventy years."

"Wow," I cried.

"After all the bombing we needed somewhere peaceful," said John. "But everywhere we liked was already taken by other ghosts. Then one day we found our perfect place, a wreck of a pirate ship, not very far from here. After we'd checked no one was haunting it, we moved in and we were so happy for a few days until It turned up."

"What's It?" I asked.

"A giant three-eyed octopus," said John.

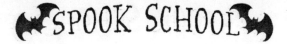

"One minute it's nowhere to be seen and the next, there it is," said Lily, "hissing and spitting. And it keeps changing colour – first it's yellow, then it's orange, next it's brown."

"Worst of all, though," said John, "is the noise it makes – a horrible, wailing cry. It makes your skin crawl."

"But you're ghosts," said Lewis. "So it can't hurt you."

"I know, but it's still so scary. And we can't share our home with it," cried Lily. "Can you make it leave?"

"Oh yeah, no problem. Dealing with scary ghosts is what we do," I replied.

"So you think it's a ghost too?" said John.

"What else could it be?" said Lewis.

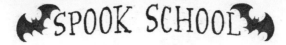

"And I've got a nose for smelling out ghosts, and I'm sure this is one," I cried. "So let's sort it."

But Lewis looked doubtful. "I'm not sure we should do this," he muttered.

"Oh, come on," I said. "We're not doing anything wrong – just helping out two ghosts."

"But we don't want Spookmaster telling us off again," said Lewis.

"Let him," I said, suddenly feeling determined. I turned to John and Lily. "Which way to the wailing octopus?"

Lily smiled. "Follow us," she said.

A few seconds later I was joined by Lewis. "Hey, I'm in charge, not you." Then he grinned. "And I've always wanted to meet an octopus."

Chapter Three

Message from an Octopus

We flew right to the end of the beach, where there were high, rocky cliffs and the sea looked grey and threatening.

"People generally avoid this part," said John. "They prefer to be where there are soft sands and ice-cream vans. And there are all sorts of stories about this wreck being haunted."

"So it's lovely and private," said Lily. "Or it was," she added sadly.

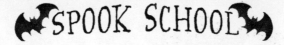

It was a dark, moonless night and both Lewis and I flew right past the pirate ship without spotting it. Well, we'd expected something big and spectacular. Instead, perched on the edge of a cliff beside an old, gnarled tree, were the mouldering remains of a very battered ship. It looked as if it had been neglected for centuries. And now it was crumbling away into the sea.

On the deck a ragged pirate flag fluttered in the breeze. And we could still make out part of the ship's figurehead: an octopus, with horrible staring eyes and fire coming out of its mouth. "Does this look like your ghost?" asked Lewis.

"Oh yes," said John.

"Only the ghost is even worse," added Lily.

There was a strange, eerie silence, too. No seagulls could be heard here. Even the sea seemed to be hushed. The only noise came from the shipwreck, which creaked away as if moaning to itself.

My voice dropped to a whisper too. "It's a bit creepy, isn't it?"

"This is John and Lily's home," hissed Lewis. "Don't be so rude."

"It's all right," said John. "I know it's a really odd place to choose. But we just feel so at home here — let us show you round."

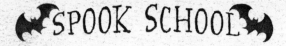

We flew down to see what was left of the cabins. The air was thick and heavy. Dust hung everywhere and spiders' webs shimmered in the deep shadows. I tried to imagine the pirates who had once lived here. Thrilling things must have happened then: daring raids and incredible sword fights, not to mention voyages to far-away islands, and quests for treasure. But all that was left of those days now was an ancient table and an old rotting chair. "I bet that was really comfortable two hundred years ago," I said.

On the wall was a portrait of a withered old pirate. He looked mean and nasty, and he had the fiercest eyebrows I'd ever seen.

"He must be the ship's captain,"
I said. "He looks nearly as grouchy as
Spookmaster."

"There are lots of stories of a strange
sea monster seen close by," said Lily. "It's
put people off coming here. Rumour has
it that no one leaves this ship alive."

"Well, that won't worry us!" Lewis
grinned.

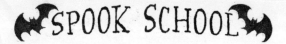

We all smiled then and Lily continued her story. "Before we moved in we checked with the senior ghost and were told no ghost has ever haunted here. Then we saw and heard the octopus."

"I bet it's one of the old pirate crew shape-changing into an octopus," I said.

"But why?" asked John.

I shrugged. "I don't know. But don't worry, we'll find out. Now what time is Mr Octopus's next appearance likely to be?"

"Oh, it can turn up at any time," said John.

"We'll wait, then," said Lewis.

So the four of us chatted away. I really liked John and Lily, and I was

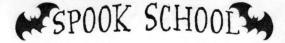

keen to help them. Far away, a clock struck midnight, but there was still no sign of the octopus.

"Maybe you two being here has scared it away," said Lily.

"Well, we have faced some pretty mean monsters in the past," I said.

"It might even have heard of us," added Lewis.

The dust and all the cobwebs were making me feel at home, as Spook School is very dusty and covered in cobwebs too. I began to see why John and Lily liked it here so much. If only it wasn't so quiet. I do like a bit of noise.

And then, quite suddenly, I heard a strange sound. Something was slithering its way along the deck.

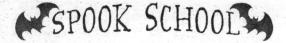

"It's here," cried Lily, her voice shaking.

"Don't worry," said Lewis, "the Spook Squad will sort it out."

"That's right," I agreed confidently. "A few seconds with us and that octopus will never bother you again. You both wait here."

Lewis and I flew up on deck, eager to confront the monster.

And then we saw it: a huge, hideous creature shuffling forward on several of its eight tentacles. Its three huge eyes were the coldest, hardest eyes I'd ever seen.

Its tentacles were writhing around as if they were trying to grab something – or someone.

36

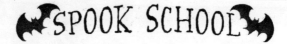

And then, out of nowhere this hair-raising wail erupted into the air. It was the loudest and most terrifying sound I'd ever heard.

"Let's get out of here," I gasped.

Lewis nodded.

We flew down on to the beach, but the terrible noise seemed to follow us. I could still hear it ringing in my ears. I thought of that massive octopus, waving its giant tentacles in the air, and a shudder ran right through me.

I saw Lewis shivering too. "It was so big," he cried.

"And evil … and as for that noise, my eardrums still haven't recovered." Then I added a bit guiltily, "We shouldn't have just flown off, though.

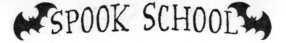

We're here to help. That's what the Spook Squad do."

"It was your idea," said Lewis.

"You didn't argue," I replied.

"I feel so ashamed," said Lewis.

"So do I," I agreed.

"And we've let Lily and John down," Lewis went on.

I thought of them, anxiously waiting for news, believing we could sort everything out. "We've got to go back," I said.

Lewis frowned. For a moment he hesitated, then he shouted, "Come on, Charlie, we can do this!"

"Of course we can!" I yelled back.

Lewis and I flew back on to the ship. The octopus was still there.

In fact, it seemed to have grown even bigger since we last saw it.

As soon as it spotted us it let out another piercing wail that sent Lewis and me rocking back. But we didn't run away this time. I gulped a few times, but I wasn't going anywhere. And neither was Lewis.

The octopus went on staring at us with its three eyes. All at once its skin changed from bright red to green.

"Who needs traffic lights when you've got an octopus?" I joked.

Lewis laughed nervously.

"So what other colours can you do?" I asked. "Do you take requests?"

Lewis stepped forward. "Hello, we're the Spook Squad. Did you know this

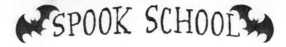

ship is already being haunted? And you're upsetting the ghosts here. So will you please leave now?" Then Lewis added politely, "Good luck in the future … I'm sure you'll find somewhere else."

The octopus made a very rude spitting sound, and then it changed colour again. Now it was orange. And suddenly there was a ghastly, gruesome stench of rotting seaweed.

"I had no idea octopuses were so smelly," I gasped. But Lewis didn't answer. He couldn't take his eyes off the terrifying creature.

"I think it's going to start wailing again," he hissed.

"Get out the earplugs," I whispered.

I half-closed my eyes to get ready for the mighty noise, but instead of a deafening shriek everything stayed eerily quiet.

"Hey," cried Lewis. "We've done it!"

My eyes shot open and I saw the

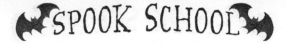

octopus had vanished. "It's gone!"
I yelled. I must have shouted really
loudly because a few moments later
John and Lily floated on to the deck.

"I can't believe you've got rid of it so
quickly," said John. "Normally it hangs
around for ages."

"And nothing we said could make it
leave," added Lily. "You're so brave!"

We weren't brave a few minutes ago,
I thought, *when we fled from the
octopus.* But, of course, neither Lewis
nor I mentioned that!

"Weren't you scared of the octopus
at all?" asked John.

"Maybe a tiny bit," I admitted. "But
Lewis and I are a good team. Have
you got any other monsters who need

scaring off?"

John grinned. "I think Spook Squad are wiz—"

But then he stopped. Lily was staring at us, her eyes glassy with horror. "It hasn't gone," she began.

"Where is it?" Lewis and I asked, ready to swing into action.

"It's left us a message," gasped Lily. "Look."

Written in the dust was one word:

BEWEAR

"Well, it's not a very good speller," I said. "I suppose it means *beware*. I'll make Mr Octopus write it out correctly ten times."

44

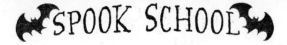

"There's more," said Lily.

"It *has* been busy," I murmured.

The second message said:

LEEVE NOW
OR ELLS

Chapter Four

The Very Last Warning

For a few seconds everyone exchanged worried looks. Then John said, "You've both been really helpful, but we can't spoil your holiday any longer. Can we, Lily?"

"No, we can't," agreed his sister. "You go off and have a wonderful time."

"But what will you two do?" I asked.

John turned to Lily. "Oh, we'll just have to look for another place to

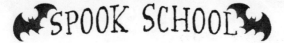

haunt." He tried to smile. "The great thing about being a ghost is you don't have any packing to do."

"But you really like it here," said Lewis.

"Yes we do," admitted John. "But—"

"But nothing," I interrupted. "We're not going to let some miserable octopus, who can't even spell properly, make you leave. We're going to stay here and fight this monster until he leaves you alone, aren't we, Lewis?"

"Yes," he agreed. "But we'd better check that Spookmaster will allow us to help first."

"I don't care what Spookmaster says," I cried, "I'm staying here. I hate bullies. And that's what this octopus is

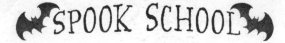

– an eight-tentacled, colour-changing, stinky bully."

"I agree," said Lewis. "But if anything goes wrong I'm the one who gets into trouble. So I'm just going to tell Spookmaster what we're doing. He's staying on Earth for a couple of days so he should be able to pick up my thoughts very easily."

Lewis flew off and reappeared a while later, looking very thoughtful. "Spookmaster says we can stay and help," he said. "But he told us to be careful because…"

"Because what?" I asked.

"Oh, nothing," said Lewis quickly. "He just told us to be careful. He also said if we can find out the name of the

ghost and why it's here that will give us power over it. And the next time the octopus appears we should shout out its real name as loudly as we can."

"Well, I bet it's the ship's captain," I said. "Who else would have their portrait on the wall?"

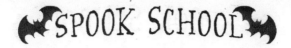

We flew down to the cabin and looked again at the portrait. "He looks like a miserable bat, doesn't he?" I said. "No, what am I saying – I like bats."

"Look," cried Lewis, pointing. "There's some tiny writing in the corner. It says *Captain Fire.*"

"Oh yes, I see it too," cried John.

"So," I said, "if it's Captain Fire who's shape-changing into an octopus, we know what to shout next time it pops by. In fact, I'll shout it now, 'Hey, Captain Fire, your ship's falling to bits and soon it'll all be in the sea – and by the way, I think you're really ugly'."

Everyone giggled.

"But why is he haunting his ship?" asked Lewis. "Perhaps he's got

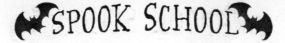

something hidden here—"

"Treasure," I interrupted. "It's got to be. Now we know the ghost's name and why he wants us to abandon ship."

"So why don't we go and look for the treasure?" asked Lewis.

"We've already searched this place from top to bottom," said Lily, "and never seen a hint of any treasure."

"Well, perhaps it got washed away … or maybe one of his crew stole it," I suggested. "We'll just have to tell smelly old Captain Fire that there's no point in him haunting the ship as there isn't any treasure."

We were all feeling really pleased with ourselves for working things out. But suddenly another message

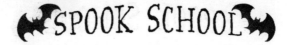

appeared. Like the others, it was
written in dust. It said:

THS IS YORR VERRY
LEST WARNNING

"'This is your very last warning',"
I translated. "Well, his spelling hasn't
got any better. I'll have to give him
a dictionary for Christmas."

"He obviously didn't like us finding
out his name and about his treasure,"
said Lily.

"Good," I cried. "That definitely
proves he's the one trying to scare
us away."

"What did he mean?" asked John.
"This is your last warning. What more
can he do to us?"

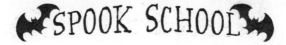

"Oh, he's just showing off," I said. "But apart from being a big nuisance, he can't do anything to us, can he, Lewis?"

For a second Lewis hesitated. Then he said, "No, he can't do anything else to us … but we should still be really careful."

Chapter Five

The Octopus Strikes

Dawn was breaking now and we were all feeling very tired, so we settled down for a nap. Then, in the afternoon, John and Lily showed us round their part of the beach – it was totally deserted apart from a few passing seagulls. The sea winked and glittered in the sun.

"It's pretty cool here," I said, swooping down to skim the waves.

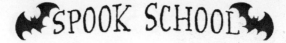

"Cool? No, I think it's quite hot today," said Lily.

I smiled. "Cool means really good."

"Oh," said Lily. "Like wizard?"

Now it was my turn to look confused. "Is that what you said back in the olden days?" I asked. "OK, it's pretty cool and dead wizard here."

As night closed in we flew back to the shipwreck. Usually this is my favourite time of day as ghosts are at their brightest. But tonight Lily and John looked super nervous. And even Lewis kept flying back and forth round the cabin.

"Just relax, everyone," I said. "I'm a million per cent certain it's going to be all right. We know the ghost's name

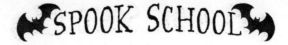

and why it's scaring everyone away. So we'll tell it there's no treasure here and to start behaving – or the Spook Squad will sort it out."

"I'm so glad you're here," Lily began, but then she stopped. "Did you just hear something move upstairs?"

Suddenly, I heard it too – a sort of squelching, shuffling sound, as if something was slithering across the deck.

"The octopus has landed," I said. "Or rather Captain Fire has. So let's go and say hello."

"Be careful," said Lewis.

"If you say that one more time I'll howl," I said. "What is the matter with you tonight?"

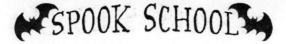

"Nothing," said Lewis, "I just think I should go up on deck alone."

"No way," I said at once. "But I think it might be best if you two wait here," I told John and Lily.

Just then, the octopus let out one of its terrible, deafening wails. The sound swept through the cabin, making the whole boat shake.

"That noise makes my knees tremble," said Lily.

"I think it's getting impatient," hissed John.

Lewis nodded. Then, to my great surprise, he actually trembled. I'd never seen him so scared before. Even I was feeling more and more nervous about this octopus. But I said as cheerfully as

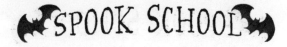

I could, "Come on, Lewis, you and I have a date with an octopus."

We floated up on deck. The octopus was crouched on its tentacles, deathly still, as if waiting to pounce. Its three eyes were fixed on us.

Lewis took a deep breath and said, "Good evening, again. Yes, it's the Spook Squad and we're here once more to ask you to stop upsetting our friends. You're not haunting this ship yourself, so leave them alone."

"And stop leaving your pathetic graffiti around too," I burst out. "And learn to spell properly."

Lewis gave me a look before going on. "We're telling you now, there's no treasure here, so leave these ghosts

alone. And we know your name…"

Lewis looked at me and we shouted
the last two words together:
"CAPTAIN FIRE!"

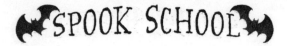

The words rippled round the old shipwreck.

The octopus changed colour from blue to the deepest yellow I'd ever seen.

It gave a vicious snarl and looked as if it were about to pounce. But instead, something really weird happened. One of the octopus's tentacles fell off. It dropped down on to the deck and lay squirming and writhing on the floor.

"It's falling apart!" I cried.

Then the tentacle began crawling across the deck.

"I've heard of all hands on deck, but this is ridiculous!" I said. All the same, I was fascinated. I moved closer to get a better look. It had turned an odd purple-black colour.

"No, Charlie!" Lewis yelled. "Get away from it."

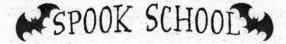

"Why?" I asked.

"Because it's a trap."

"A trap? What are you—" But I never finished my sentence. One of the octopus's other tentacles swung into action like a vicious snake grabbing its prey. Before I knew what was happening it had yanked hold of me, and I went spinning up into the air.

At first I was annoyed rather than frightened. "Very funny, Captain Fire," I said, trying to break free.

But the octopus had only just started. Suddenly, it began firing what looked like black goo at me from one of its other tentacles. Great torrents of it rained over me. It was warm and sticky and it hung on me like tar.

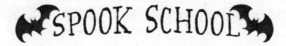

"Lewis, help!" I cried.

But instead Lewis yelled, "Oh no!"

He sounded so scared he frightened me too. I knew I had to break free, but no matter how hard I wriggled I couldn't get away from the creature's vice-like grip. "You may think you're scaring me, but you're not," I shrieked, my voice sounding thin and scratchy.

Then I decided I'd just vanish. Any spook can normally do this in a couple of seconds, and I'm the best in my class. But suddenly my powers had deserted me. I couldn't disappear. I couldn't do anything. I was completely trapped.

I tried to call out to Lewis to help, but somehow the words wouldn't come. The octopus had crushed every ounce

of my strength, and all the time I was getting covered in more black goo.

Suddenly, Lewis yelled, "Stop it! I'm the leader, so you should be attacking me, not him."

Lewis flew up to the octopus, his whole body trembling with fear. "Stop this now, Captain Fire – or else."

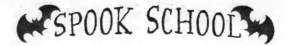

Then he added, "Charlie, are you all right?"

"Oh yeah, I can hardly move." But somehow I managed to croak, "Best holiday I've ever had."

All at once, the octopus's tentacle – the one holding me very tightly – soared above its head and launched me into the air. It was as if I'd been shot out of a cannon. Petrified with fear, I rocketed into the sky. I flew through the shipwreck, and hurtled down on to the sand below.

I lay there shivering and shaking, with black goo oozing down my face.

Lewis rushed over. "Charlie, Charlie! Are you all right? Say something!"

I opened and shut my mouth.

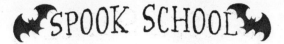

SPOOK SCHOOL

"Hello," I said at last.

Then John and Lily came flying down to the beach too. "Oh no," cried Lily. "Poor Charlie, what's happened to him?"

"Yeah, Lewis, what's happened to me?" I managed to splutter.

"I'm afraid," said Lewis, "you've just been whooshed."

Chapter Six

All about Whooshing

"Whooshed?" I stared up at Lewis. "What's that?"

"I've never heard of it," said John.

"Most ghosts don't know about whooshing," said Lewis. "But then most don't have to deal with bad ghosts. Spookmaster says there are a few real bad 'uns out there, who whoosh. And he feared the octopus, otherwise known as Captain Fire, might be one of them."

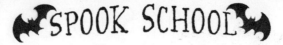

"And he certainly is," murmured Lily.

Lewis went on. "To protect all other ghosts, a few spooks learn how to fight back against the black goo by whooshing too. That black goo has the power to freeze ghosts, and that's what's happened to you, hasn't it, Charlie?"

I nodded grimly.

"And it makes you feel as if you've got really bad flu too, doesn't it?"

I nodded again, and then croaked, "I feel awful."

"Oh, poor Charlie," said Lily. "I do think you're very brave."

"And so do I," said John.

"Well," said Lewis, "the good news is the symptoms should only last a few hours."

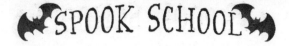

"A few hours," I moaned. "But why didn't you tell me about this whooshing before, Lewis?"

He lowered his head. "Spookmaster told me not to."

"But I'm your best friend," I said.

Lewis's face reddened. "I wanted to tell you so badly," he said, "but Spookmaster made me promise. He said whooshing is such a terrible thing to do to a fellow ghost. And if Captain Fire didn't whoosh anyone," his voice fell away, "well, there would be no need for you to know about it."

"You still should have told me."

"Look," interrupted John, "let's get you back inside the ship. Can you still fly all right, Charlie?"

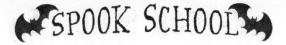

"Oh yeah," I began. I stumbled to my feet and launched myself into the air. But instead of going up I just lurched about in all directions. It was so funny that I had to laugh. At last I zigzagged my way towards the shipwreck.

"Let me go first," said Lewis, "just in case the octopus is still lurking about. Not that I think he will be," he added hastily.

And he wasn't.

I sat huddled in the cabin, still unable to stop shaking.

Lewis kept giving me anxious looks.

"Feeling guilty, are you?" I asked.

"I'll never keep anything secret from you again," he said.

"I don't believe you," I snapped. "You'd do anything to be Spookmaster's little pet."

"No, I wouldn't."

"Yes you would," I cried. "Just leave me alone." I felt ill, grumpy and very, very tired.

"Try and get some sleep," said Lily,
floating over to us.

"I feel so ill, I shan't sleep a wink,"
I moaned.

Two seconds later I fell fast asleep.
I didn't wake up until the middle of the
afternoon. As soon as I stirred, Lewis,
Lily and John hovered
round me anxiously.

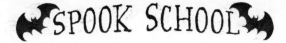

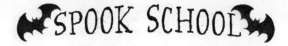

"How are you feeling?" asked Lewis.

I stretched and then gave a sigh of relief. "I've stopped shaking," I said. "And I'm all clean again too." Then I remembered that I was still angry with Lewis so I just scowled up at him.

Lewis looked upset for a moment and then said, "Well, now you're all right, I'd better go and speak to Spookmaster, and tell him what's happened. I'll ask him if he'll teach me how to whoosh."

"Oh no," said Lily. "Do you really need to?"

Lewis nodded. "When Captain Fire comes back we've got to be able to defend ourselves."

"What about me?" I asked.

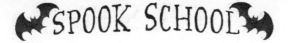

"I'll teach you how to whoosh as well, I promise," said Lewis. "But you need to rest now. So just stretch out on deck — and leave everything to me. OK?"

I sort of nodded.

After he'd left, Lily said, "I feel so guilty putting you and Lewis to all this trouble."

"Well, don't," I said, as we made our way up on deck. "And don't worry, we won't leave until we've sorted out Captain Fire, once and for all."

When we got there we found yet another message. This one said:

NO MER
WARNNINGS
LEEVE NOOW

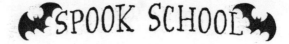

"'No more warnings leave now'," I read. "He's such a friendly guy, really makes you feel welcome."

"He wants us away from this ship so badly, doesn't he?" said John.

"Yes," I said, thinking for a moment. "I know you've already searched the ship, but he's got to have buried the treasure here somewhere. Let's have one last search for it."

The three of us flew round every corner of the old ship, but there was no sign of treasure anywhere. "It's definitely not on the ship," said Lily at last. "We've looked all over."

"But it won't be very far away," I said.

I decided to have another think about this on the beach. But just as I

was leaving the shipwreck, I noticed the old, gnarled tree again. It had probably been there for hundreds of years – maybe even before the wreck.

And right then I had a brilliant brainwave. I reckoned I knew exactly where Captain Fire had buried his treasure…

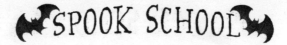

I whizzed back inside the shipwreck. "Guess what," I cried. "I think I know where the treasure's hidden — beneath that ancient tree outside."

John and Lily stared at me for a moment, and then John exclaimed, "By Jove, you could be right."

Lily's eyes shone with fear. "Wouldn't Captain Fire be mad if someone found his treasure?" she asked.

"Yes, but he'd also have no reason to scare us away any more," said John.

"You're right, he wouldn't," I said. "But there's just one problem. Being ghosts, we can't dig it up."

John sighed. "Maybe Lewis will know what to do when he gets back."

This really irritated me. "I'll tell you

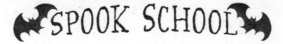

what Lewis will do," I said huffily.
"He'll just fly off to Spookmaster again.
He can't think for himself. I'm the
brains of the team, you know."

"So what do you suggest?" asked
Lily, looking at me hopefully.

I hadn't expected that! I started
to think so hard I thought I'd burst.
"I know," I cried at last. "I'll go and find
a human to dig up the treasure for us."

"Could you do that?" asked Lily,
impressed.

"Yeah, sure. Just leave it to me,"
I said, enjoying Lily and John's look of
admiration. "I'll bring a human back
with me, no problem."

Neither of them guessed I hadn't a
clue what I was going to do next.

Chapter Seven
The Talking Seashell

When you're a bit of a show-off – like me – you get yourself into difficult situations sometimes. But this was my toughest one yet.

Could I really wander up to a human and say, "Excuse me, but I'm a ghost and I need you to do a bit of digging. So grab a spade and follow me."

I groaned. I couldn't see *that* happening. But I flew off towards the

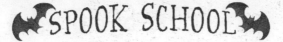

main part of the beach, hoping I'd get inspiration when I got there.

Although it was late afternoon it was still pretty crowded. It had been another warm day, and the sun beamed down on everyone, while the sea glistened invitingly. I still hadn't had a better idea, so I looked around for someone about my age to approach. They'd be more likely to believe in ghosts. But who?

All the children seemed to be in groups: some were with their parents, so they were ruled out right away. Others were in gangs, building sandcastles and playing games. I felt a bit shy about explaining myself to so many people at once. I wanted to

appear to just one child, on his or her own. Then I spotted him. He was standing alone, shouting at some other children, "I don't want to play with any of you, anyway. You all smell. I hate every one of you."

I recognized that voice at once. It was Andrew, the boy who'd been so rude about ghosts at the fair. He wasn't someone I'd normally have chosen to help me in a crisis, but he was the only child on his own. And time was running out.

Suddenly, I remembered that Spookmaster had told us we mustn't appear to humans except in emergencies. But this was an emergency, wasn't it? Anyway, I'd

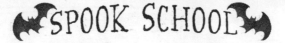

already got us into trouble for
appearing to Andrew – so we couldn't
be told off for it twice, could we?

So I said, "See me, Andrew" twice,
and flew over to say hello.

He was searching about on the
beach for some seashells when I
appeared. I stood in front of him.

"Hi, Andrew."

He put down his shells and stared
up at me. "I don't know you."

"Yes, you do," I said. "We met at the
fair. I'm Charlie, the ghost."

Andrew's eyes practically popped
out of his head. "You're not real," he
gasped at last.

"Oh yes, I am," I said. "Watch."
I turned two somersaults.

"No," said Andrew, shaking his head. "I'm imagining you again, because I've got such an exceptional imagination."

"Oh, don't be like that, Andrew," I said. "Most people would love to hang out with a ghost. Can't we be friends?"

"No, we can't." He picked up his shells. "You're going to vanish now."

"Oh no I'm not."

"Yes, you are – bye, bye."

"Look, Andrew…" I began.

"No, I'm ignoring you until you disappear."

"Andrew, I wouldn't bother you normally, but I need your help. So come on, talk to me."

Andrew shook his head and stared down at the shells.

I sighed with frustration and decided to seize his attention by shape-changing into a shell. I pictured the shell in my head, concentrating really hard, and then I vanished.

"Phew!" cried Andrew, "I'm glad he's gone." But the very next shell Andrew picked up spoke to him.

"Hi, Andrew," it said, "been quite hot today, hasn't it?"

Andrew stared at the shell, as if he were hypnotized by it.

Then he saw my eyes peering up at him, and dropped the shell as if it had just bitten him.

"Now don't be alarmed," I called up at him. "It's me again, your friendly local ghost."

"But how did you become a shell?"

"Oh, I shape-changed. I learned to do that in the first term at Spook School. Nothing to it really. But I'll

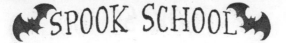

change back to my normal shape now."

And in a flash, I did just that. "Ah that's better," I said, grinning at him.

"Can anyone else see you?" asked Andrew.

"No, just you … I picked you specially, for a top-secret mission."

"You picked me?" said Andrew. And he couldn't keep a note of pride out of his voice.

"That's right. And I really do need your help."

"The thing is, I'm not all that keen on helping people," admitted Andrew. "Or ghosts."

"Oh, you'll like this mission – it's to find some treasure."

That got Andrew's attention all

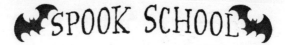

right, but then he frowned. "How do I know you're telling me the truth?"

I thought for a moment. "Why are ghosts bad liars?"

"I don't know."

"Because you can see right through them. Get it?" I started to laugh, and to my surprise Andrew laughed too.

Then he said, "Tell me more about this treasure…"

Chapter Eight

Treasure?

Just a few minutes later, Andrew and I were on our way to the shipwreck. Andrew was so excited he hadn't even tried to borrow a spade. ("Too many questions and my cousins might want to come along too," he said.) Instead, he'd bought a new one from the seaside shop.

Andrew told me his parents had had to go away for a few weeks, leaving him

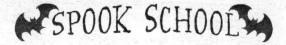

to go on holiday with his uncle and aunt and four cousins. "I don't fit in with any of them," he said sadly. "They just think I'm a big nuisance."

"So now you're *acting* like a big nuisance," I said. "I don't blame you."

Andrew looked across at me. "I'm not normally so rude. Honestly. But I thought if they don't want me around, why should I act all nice with them?"

When we got to the rocks I said, "Now don't rush and fall."

But Andrew clambered over the rocks with surprising skill. It was only when we reached the shipwreck that he hesitated. "There are all sorts of stories about this place," he said, his voice starting to shake.

"I know, but you won't have to go inside," I said.

"But what if the spooky things come outside," he replied.

"Look, the only ghosts haunting this shipwreck are two children, about your age. But this nasty pirate ghost disguised as an octopus keeps turning up trying to scare them away. We think he's guarding his treasure. If we can

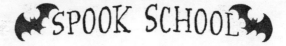

find it he might finally leave them alone. And anything you find is yours. So come on, I'll watch out for you – just get digging."

"OK. I hope we find tons of treasure," said Andrew. "And I hope the octopus doesn't show up." Then he got to work. He didn't see the three other ghosts watching him. But, of course, I did.

John, Lily and Lewis came floating out of the shipwreck.

"I'll be back soon, Andrew," I said.

A little way away from Andrew I faced a very angry Lewis. "What's going on?" he demanded.

"I think I've worked out where the treasure is and Andrew's going to dig it up."

"But why didn't you wait until I got back?" said Lewis.

"Well, I didn't know how long you'd be chatting with your very great mate, Spookmaster. I expect you're his top pet now, aren't you?"

Lewis didn't answer, just flew round and round in a circle, frowning.

"What are you doing?" I asked.

"Trying to control my temper," he snapped. "You can be so annoying."

"Not as annoying as you," I replied. "Anyway, did you find out how to whoosh?"

"Yes, and I've got Spookmaster's permission to whoosh Captain Fire, if it looks like he's going to attack us."

"What about me?" I asked at once.

Lewis paused.

"Oh, don't tell me. I'm not allowed."

Lewis gave me a lopsided grin. "Of course you're allowed … I just have to tell you how!"

Suddenly, Andrew let out a loud cry. "Hey, Charlie, I've found something."

I was beside Andrew in a zillionth of a second. He was holding a wooden chest in his hands. It was covered in mud and maggots, tons and tons of them, wriggling and squirming all over the place. But Andrew hardly noticed them. For this had to be it: the treasure.

"I bet it's locked," he said, but after a bit of tugging the lid creaked open.

We both looked inside to see, not diamonds or jewels or pieces of gold, but just … well, once it must have been crammed with paper money, thousands, maybe millions of pounds' worth of it.

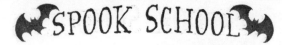

But over
the years the
paper money
had all
dissolved away,
and now all that
was left was a
mouldy, gooey mess.

Andrew looked
down at it in dismay. "What a let-down," he said. "It's all gone."

"I'm sorry," I said, "really sorry."

Andrew examined the box. "Look," he cried, pointing at the tiny holes in the bottom of the box, "fancy hoarding all your money in a box with holes in it. That pirate wasn't exactly clever, was he?" Then Andrew smiled. "Been an

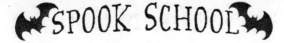

adventure, though. In fact, it's the only bit of this holiday I've enjoyed." He sighed. "I suppose I'd better be getting back now – just in case anyone has missed me."

"Well, take the box anyway," I said. "And thanks for finding the treasure – I hope your holiday gets better now."

Andrew smiled. "For a ghost, you're all right."

"And you're all right too," I said.

"So," said Lewis, after Andrew had gone. "Captain Fire has been madly guarding his money box all these years – when actually, it's completely worthless."

He started to laugh and we all joined in. We were still laughing as

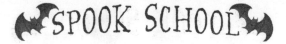

we flew back into the cabin.

I even started calling out things like, "Hey, Captain Fire, want to borrow a fiver?" We were all having fun when suddenly a great wail tore through the shipwreck.

"It's him," shrieked Lily at once.

"And I don't think he liked us laughing at him," said John.

I looked at Lewis. "Perhaps now would be a good time to tell me how to whoosh."

"There are different ways, but the one Spookmaster taught me is this," said Lewis. "First of all, you wave your hand round twice. Then you point your forefinger and say, 'Whoosh fire' twice. Got it?"

Before I could reply, Lily cried,
"What's that?"

A grey, cloudy shape was oozing
into the cabin. It hung heavily in the
air like a dark cloud, smelling very
strongly of seaweed.

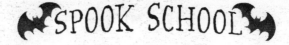

Captain Fire was back. Only this time he hadn't shape-changed into an octopus. He was appearing as himself. And very slowly, very confidently, as if enjoying our shocked reaction, the figure of Captain Fire formed in front of us.

He was a hideous sight. First there was the captain's hat, with a skull and crossbones on, and then came those thick, jagged eyebrows we'd seen in his portrait, and the dark, ferociously fierce eyes. But the portrait had missed out his scars, which hung heavily down both sides of his face. And while his mouth looked angry in the portrait, now it was twisted with rage as he loomed in front of us.

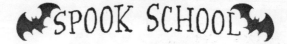

"Actually," I said, "I think you looked better when you were an octopus. And I'm really sorry about your loot. Which is now money-stew."

Lily let out a nervous laugh.

"No one laughs at me," he hissed. If ever a snake spoke, I bet it would sound exactly like Captain Fire.

"Let's see if you'll still be laughing after this," he went on. He flashed a cruel smile, displaying all his chipped, dark brown teeth. His hand swung wildly in the air, then he pointed his fat forefinger – not at me – but at Lily.

"Oh no you don't," I cried, determined to whoosh Captain Fire first. I pointed my finger right at his head, said, "Whoosh fire", twice – and nothing happened.

Luckily, Lewis had more success, and soon black goo was zooming out of his finger and straight in Captain Fire's direction. But the Captain ducked sharply and glided out of

103

the way. For such a big ghost he could move very fast. Still, at least Lewis had stopped him whooshing Lily.

Captain Fire's next target was me. Lewis shouted out a warning and the black goo almost splattered in my face,

but I swerved out of danger just in time. "Never touched me," I yelled. Then I whispered to Lewis, "I can't whoosh him back, what's happening?"

Lewis whispered, "Did you wave your arms about first?"

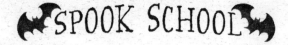

"Oh no, I forgot that bit," I said.

There was no time to say anything else, as Captain Fire was shooting black gunge off in all directions. Lily gave a terrified whimper. And John was shaking with fear.

I glanced at Lewis. He nodded. We took careful aim and then, with lightning speed, we fired together. This time we scored a bull's eye. Lewis hit Captain Fire right on the chin. And I got him just above his nose. Thick black liquid gushed all the way down his face. Captain Fire gave a furious bellow of frustration. But the black goo meant he couldn't move. He just hung there in the air like a big, fat cloud.

Then I had a brilliant idea. I concentrated hard and said, "Captain Fire, go soaring off to the beach."

At once, the old pirate was lifted high up into the air, as if he were on an invisible fairground ride.

The next moment he blasted off. We all cheered and flew after him as he bounced down on to the sand.

There he lay, groaning and wheezing like a great beached whale.

Chapter Ten
Facing Captain Fire

John and Lily hung back. "Don't worry," I said. "He can't do anything to you now. We've zapped his powers." I flew right right up to him. He was shaking and covered in black goo.

"Glad you're getting a taste of your own medicine," I said.

Captain Fire glared up at Lewis and me. "I'll get you for this," he rumbled.

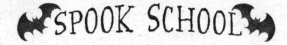

"No you won't," said Lewis, "because we'll just get you again – and the whole thing is totally pointless, really, considering you haven't got any treasure now."

"You laughed at me," hissed Captain Fire, baring his rotten, brown teeth. "No one ever does that." He tried to haul himself up, but it was no use. He floundered helplessly and gave a howl of fury.

"Look, you've got to admit, it was pretty funny," I said, "you guarding money that had all been washed away years ago. Perhaps you should have a laugh about it," I chortled. "There's nothing like a good joke, is there?".

Captain Fire's shrivelled old eyes flashed with rage and he gave a deep snarl. I'd just made him even angrier.

Lewis gave me an *I'll sort this out* look.

"Now listen to me, Captain Fire," he said. "Your treasure has gone, so you have no reason to bother these two ghosts any more. It's time to leave your ship for ever."

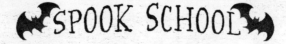

"No one tells me what to do," cried Captain Fire.

"The Spook Squad do," said Lewis very firmly. I felt quite proud of him at that moment. "So will you go quietly?" he asked. "Or do you want another battle?"

Captain Fire didn't answer. He just lay there, growling and shivering.

Then all at once a thin mist started to form around him, and there was a deathly silence as his body began to ooze away. Soon the only things left were his great, black beard, still covered in sticky black goo, and his fierce scowling eyes.

"Bye then," I called. "Oh, are you on Facebook?"

John and Lily looked confused, but Lewis burst out laughing. "You're nearly as mad as him," he said, pointing at the nearly-vanished Captain Fire. Then all that remained was a tiny speck of grey cloud. We watched it disappear into the dark night.

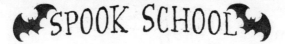

"Hey, we saw him off, didn't we?" I said.

"We certainly did," agreed Lewis. And now there was nothing left of Captain Fire at all, except a faint stench of stale seaweed.

"He really should use deodorant," I muttered. "Perhaps I should try and send him some."

Then Lewis turned to John and Lily. "I don't think Captain Fire will ever bother you again."

The next afternoon we had a visitor –
Andrew. He hung around outside the
shipwreck, calling, "Hey, ghost-boy,
Charlie. Are you there?"

A few seconds later I materialized
in front of him. Andrew looked very
excited. "Guess what … there might
not have been any treasure inside that
box, but the box itself is really valuable,
even though it's got holes in it.

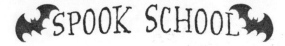

SPOOK SCHOOL

My uncle's going up to London to have it valued tomorrow. And he thinks I might get a big reward from a museum. Of course no one understands how I found the box. I didn't give you away."

"Well done," I said.

"But I wanted to say thank you. I'm a bit of a hero right now, and everyone wants to talk to me – even my cousins."

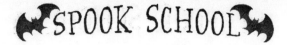

I grinned. "So you're a big nuisance no longer."

"Thanks to you," said Andrew. "Come back and haunt me any time you like."

Then came the second surprise. Lewis and I were chatting on the deck, when who should appear in front of us, but Spookmaster.

"Wow! Seeing you is nearly as scary as Captain Fire," I joked.

Did a flicker of a smile cross Spookmaster's face? Hard to tell as he flew right up into the air, his cloak flapping about. "I just wanted to let you both know that I think you did very well. And I'm impressed that you gave up your holiday to help Lily and John."

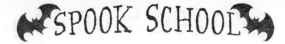

"I really liked helping them," I said quietly.

"So did I," said Lewis.

"There's good in both of you," said Spookmaster. "Yes, even you, Charlie – somewhere. And so I shall count the last few nights as work – your two-week holiday starts now."

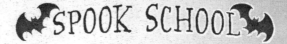

Before either of us could reply, he'd vanished.

"What about that?" said Lewis. "You know, I reckon if anyone is Spookmaster's pet, it's you."

"Rubbish," I muttered, hoping I wasn't going red.

Then Lily and John flew up on deck. "We'd both really like it if you stayed with us a bit longer, as our guests," said Lily. "And we can go to the fair every single night, if you like."

"Sounds brilliant," I said, looking at Lewis, who was nodding enthusiastically.

"So come on, everyone," I yelled, "let's go and have some fun."

OUT NOW:

PETE JOHNSON

SPOOK SCHOOL

LAIR OF THE MOTHMAN

Charlie isn't happy when he finds out he's a spook and he still has to go to school ... until he discovers lessons include flying through walls and making objects move!

But are Charlie and his new friend, Lewis, ready to join Spook Squad? Their first secret mission is to investigate Mothman – a terrifying creature with deadly claws, an even deadlier smell and a very bad temper...

OUT NOW:

PETE JOHNSON

SPOOK SCHOOL

Curse of the Rat-beast

Charlie loves being a spook and he can't wait for his next Spook Squad mission, but it's going to be his most baffling investigation yet!

A giant rat is haunting a boy down on Earth – it's a terrifying creature, which can expand to the size of a pony. Charlie and his best friend, Lewis, must find out what this sinister rat is up to and get it to stop … but they're in for a massive shock!

Jokes
(FOR PIRATE FOLK)
What did the pirate say when his wooden leg got stuck in the freezer?
Shiver me timbers!

Find out more about Pete Johnson at:

www.petejohnsonauthor.com